D0118673

THE NEXT STEP IN HUMAN EVOLUTION HAS ARRIVED—HOMO SUPERIOR. MANKIND ISN'T SURE WHETHER THIS REPRESENTS HOPE FOR THE FUTURE...OR THE END OF THE HUMAN RACE. IN A PRIVATE SCHOOL IN UPSTATE NEW YORK, ONE BRILLIANT MUTANT IS TEACHING A GROUP OF FIVE SUCH GIFTED STUDENTS WHAT THEY'LL NEED TO SURVIVE IN THIS NEW WORLD. THESE ARE THE UNTOLD STORIES OF PROFESSOR XAVIER'S FIRST CLASS OF X-MEN!

XAVIER'S SCHOOL FOR GIFTED YOUNGSTERS

PROPERTY OF:

CYCLOPS

a life of the mind

HEADMASTER

WHY DID I LET THE PROF PICK MY NAME? I DO KIND OF LIKE IT WHEN THE GUYS CALL ME CYKE THOUGH...

BOY, I HAVEN'T CALLED ALEX IN A WHILE--WONDER IF HE'S TAKING CARE OF MY CAR.

PROFESSOR CHARLES XAVIER

I SEE EVERYTHING AS RED. JEAN HAS RED HAIR. COINCIDENCE? FATE?

GOT TO THANK HANK FOR LENDING SUN TZU'S THE ART OF WAR. FINALLY HE RECOMMENDS SOMETHING I UNDERSTAND.

SCOTT SUMMERS
"CYCLOPS"

JEAN GREY
"MARVEL GIRL"

HENRY "HANK" MCCOY
"BEAST"

COULD FLY LIKE WARREN, I ULD TARGET THREATS SO MUCH ETTER... OF COURSE I MIGHT BARF ON THEM TOO. I DON'T KNOW HOW HE CAN MANEUVER LIKE THAT WITHOUT LOSING IT.

WARREN WORTHINGTON III
"ANGEL"

ROBERT DRAKE
"ICEMAN"

THERMOSTAT IN ROOM NOT BROKEN, BOBBY IS JUST PRANKING ME AGAIN. LITTLE #&^!@

WHEN IS THAT JET GOING TO BE FINISHED? VERTICAL TAKE-OFF AND LANDING, SPEED OF SOUND... NOW THAT'S A PROPER SUPER HERO RIDE.

WRITER
JEFF PARKER

PENCILER
ROGER CRUZ

INKER
VICTOR OLAZABA

COVER ARTIST
MARKO DJURDJEVIC

LETTERER
NATE PIEKOS

COLORIST
VAL STAPLES

PRODUCTION
KATE LEVIN

ASSISTANT EDITOR
NATHAN COSBY

EDITOR
MARK PANICCIA

EDITOR IN CHIEF
JOE QUESADA

PUBLISHER
DAN BUCKLEY

Spotlight

MARVEL

VISIT US AT
www.abdopublishing.com

Reinforced library bound edition published in 2008 by Spotlight, a division of the ABDO Publishing Group, 8000 West 78th Street, Edina, Minnesota 55439. Spotlight produces high-quality reinforced library bound editions for schools and libraries. Published by agreement with Marvel Characters, Inc.

Library of Congress Cataloging-in-Publication Data

Parker, Jeff, 1966-
A life of the mind / writer, Jeff Parker ; penciler, Roger Cruz ; inker, Victor Olazaba ; cover artist, Marko Djurdjevic letterer, Nate Piekos ; colorist, Val Staples. -- Reinforced library bound ed.
p. cm. -- (X-men)
"Marvel age"--Cover.
Revision of issue 3 of X-Men.
ISBN 978-1-59961-399-4
1. Graphic novels. I. Cruz, Roger. II. X-Men (New York, N.Y. : 2004). 3. III. Title.

PN6728.X2P37 2008
741.5'973--dc22

2007020244

All Spotlight books have reinforced library bindings and are manufactured in the United States of America.

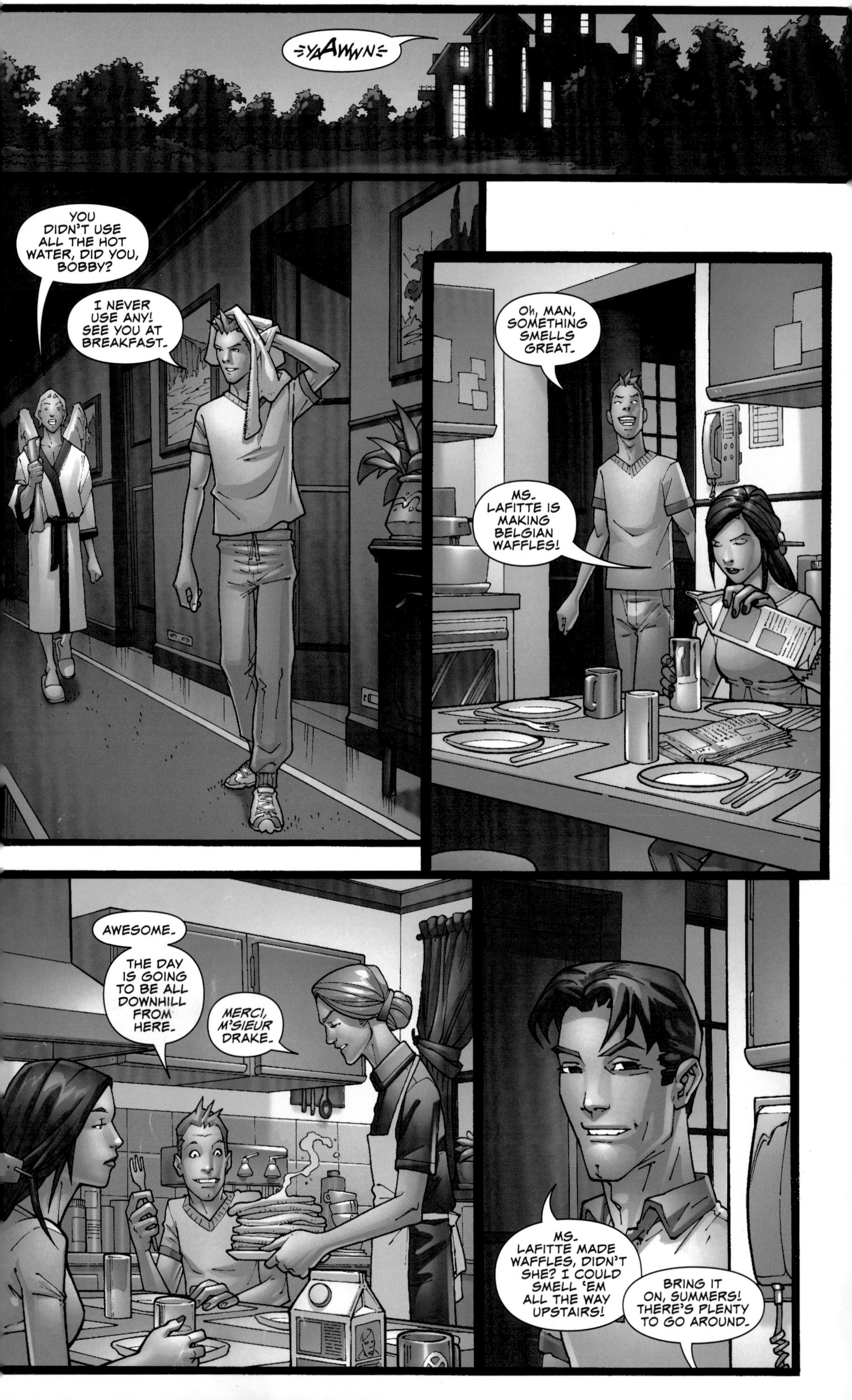

YAAWWN
YOU DIDN'T USE ALL THE HOT WATER, DID YOU, BOBBY?
I NEVER USE ANY! SEE YOU AT BREAKFAST.
OH, MAN, SOMETHING SMELLS GREAT.
MS. LAFITTE IS MAKING BELGIAN WAFFLES!
AWESOME.
THE DAY IS GOING TO BE ALL DOWNHILL FROM HERE.
MERCI, M'SIEUR DRAKE.
MS. LAFITTE MADE WAFFLES, DIDN'T SHE? I COULD SMELL 'EM ALL THE WAY UPSTAIRS!
BRING IT ON, SUMMERS! THERE'S PLENTY TO GO AROUND.

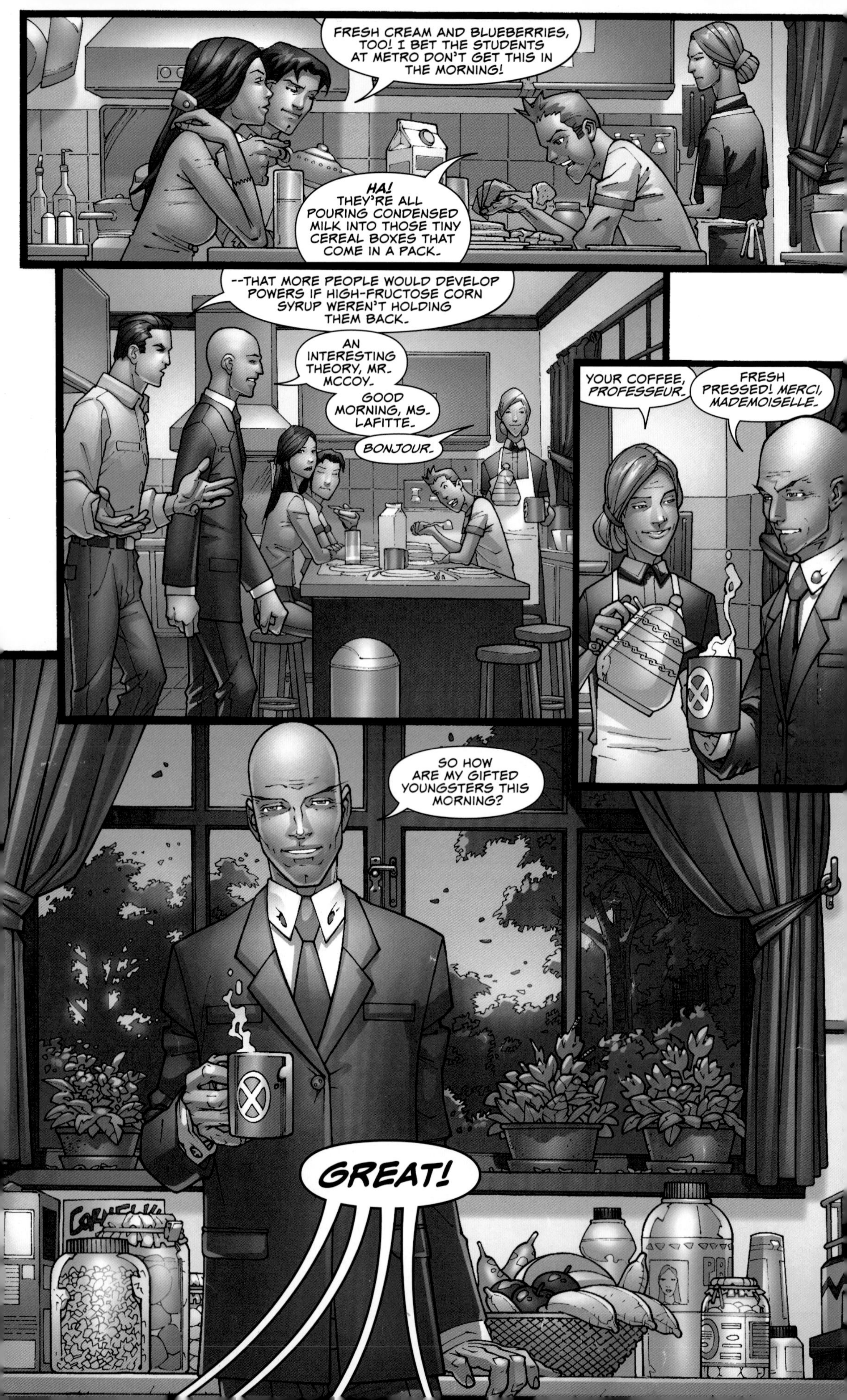
FRESH CREAM AND BLUEBERRIES, TOO! I BET THE STUDENTS AT METRO DON'T GET THIS IN THE MORNING!
HA! THEY'RE ALL POURING CONDENSED MILK INTO THOSE TINY CEREAL BOXES THAT COME IN A PACK.
--THAT MORE PEOPLE WOULD DEVELOP POWERS IF HIGH-FRUCTOSE CORN SYRUP WEREN'T HOLDING THEM BACK.
AN INTERESTING THEORY, MR. MCCOY.
GOOD MORNING, MS. LAFITTE.
BONJOUR.
YOUR COFFEE, PROFESSEUR.
FRESH PRESSED! MERCI, MADEMOISELLE.
SO HOW ARE MY GIFTED YOUNGSTERS THIS MORNING?
GREAT!

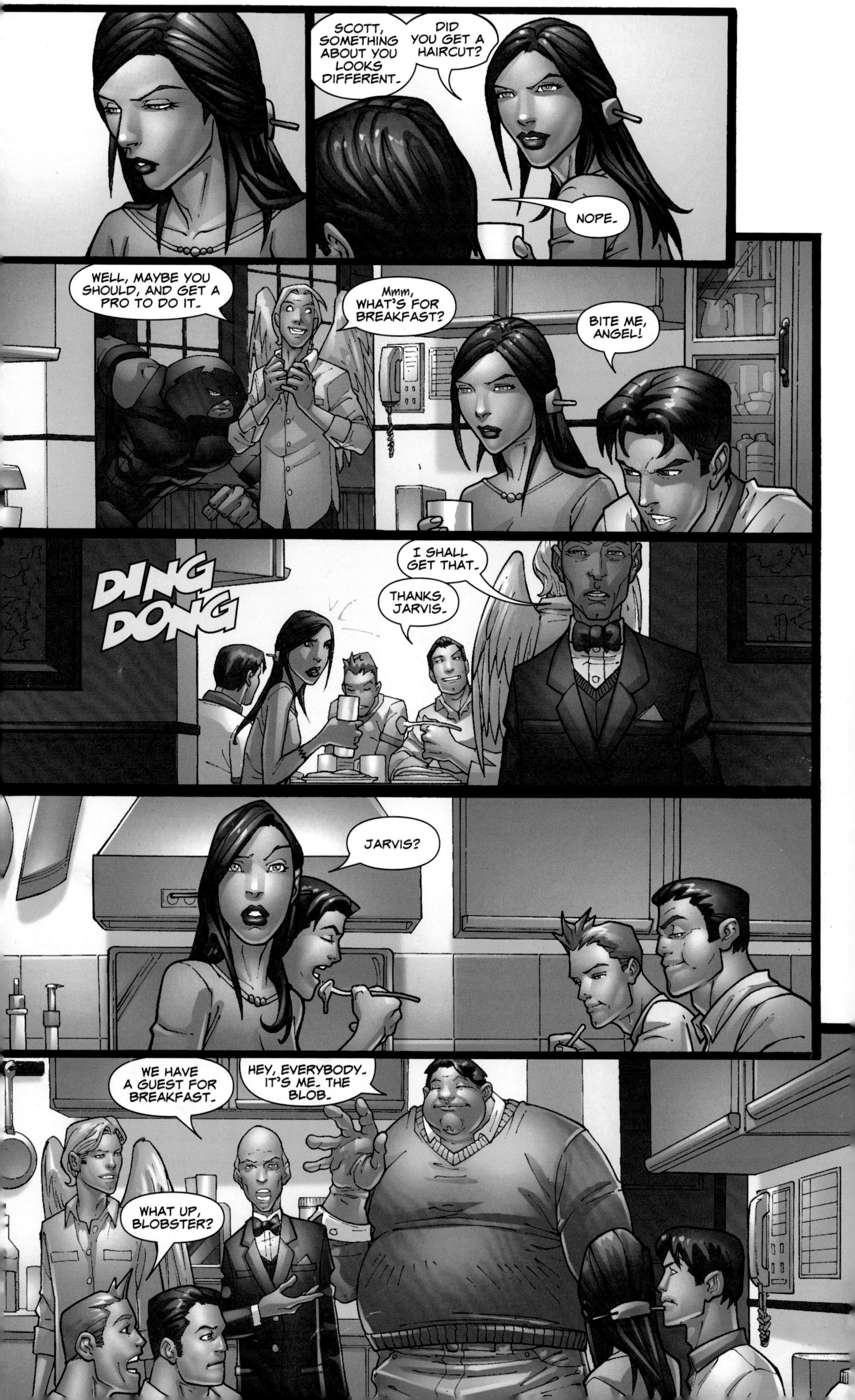
SCOTT, SOMETHING ABOUT YOU LOOKS DIFFERENT.
DID YOU GET A HAIRCUT?
NOPE.
WELL, MAYBE YOU SHOULD, AND GET A PRO TO DO IT.
Mmm, WHAT'S FOR BREAKFAST?
BITE ME, ANGEL!
DING DONG
I SHALL GET THAT.
THANKS, JARVIS.
JARVIS?
WE HAVE A GUEST FOR BREAKFAST.
HEY, EVERYBODY. IT'S ME. THE BLOB.
WHAT UP, BLOBSTER?

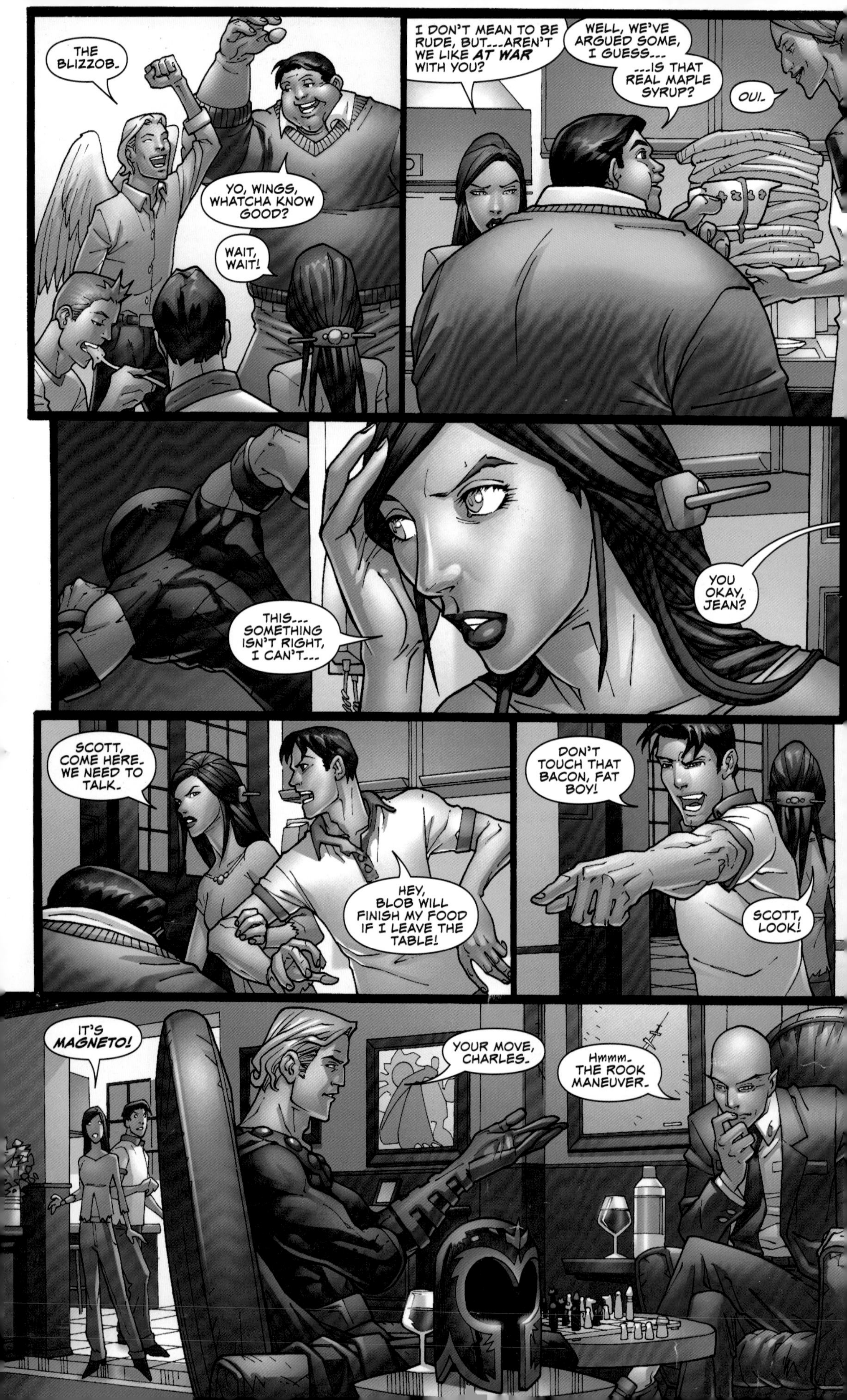
THE BLIZZOB.
YO, WINGS, WHATCHA KNOW GOOD?
WAIT, WAIT!
I DON'T MEAN TO BE RUDE, BUT... AREN'T WE LIKE AT WAR WITH YOU?
WELL, WE'VE ARGUED SOME, I GUESS...
...IS THAT REAL MAPLE SYRUP?
OUI.
THIS... SOMETHING ISN'T RIGHT, I CAN'T...
YOU OKAY, JEAN?
SCOTT, COME HERE. WE NEED TO TALK.
HEY, BLOB WILL FINISH MY FOOD IF I LEAVE THE TABLE!
DON'T TOUCH THAT BACON, FAT BOY!
SCOTT, LOOK!
IT'S MAGNETO!
YOUR MOVE, CHARLES.
Hmmm. THE ROOK MANEUVER.

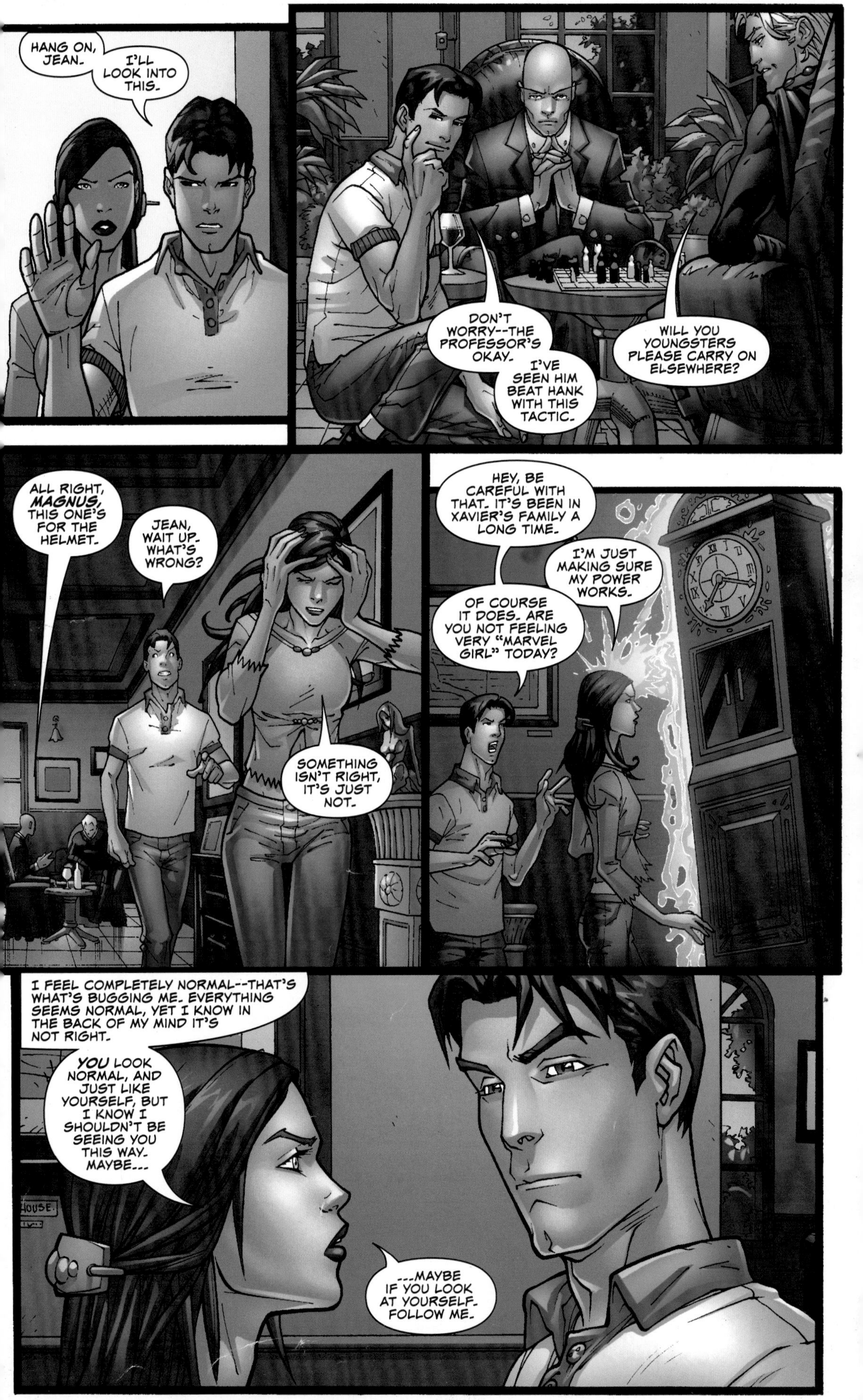
HANG ON, JEAN.
I'LL LOOK INTO THIS.
DON'T WORRY--THE PROFESSOR'S OKAY.
I'VE SEEN HIM BEAT HANK WITH THIS TACTIC.
WILL YOU YOUNGSTERS PLEASE CARRY ON ELSEWHERE?
ALL RIGHT, MAGNUS, THIS ONE'S FOR THE HELMET.
JEAN, WAIT UP. WHAT'S WRONG?
SOMETHING ISN'T RIGHT, IT'S JUST NOT.
HEY, BE CAREFUL WITH THAT. IT'S BEEN IN XAVIER'S FAMILY A LONG TIME.
I'M JUST MAKING SURE MY POWER WORKS.
OF COURSE IT DOES. ARE YOU NOT FEELING VERY "MARVEL GIRL" TODAY?
I FEEL COMPLETELY NORMAL--THAT'S WHAT'S BUGGING ME. EVERYTHING SEEMS NORMAL, YET I KNOW IN THE BACK OF MY MIND IT'S NOT RIGHT.
YOU LOOK NORMAL, AND JUST LIKE YOURSELF, BUT I KNOW I SHOULDN'T BE SEEING YOU THIS WAY. MAYBE...
...MAYBE IF YOU LOOK AT YOURSELF. FOLLOW ME.

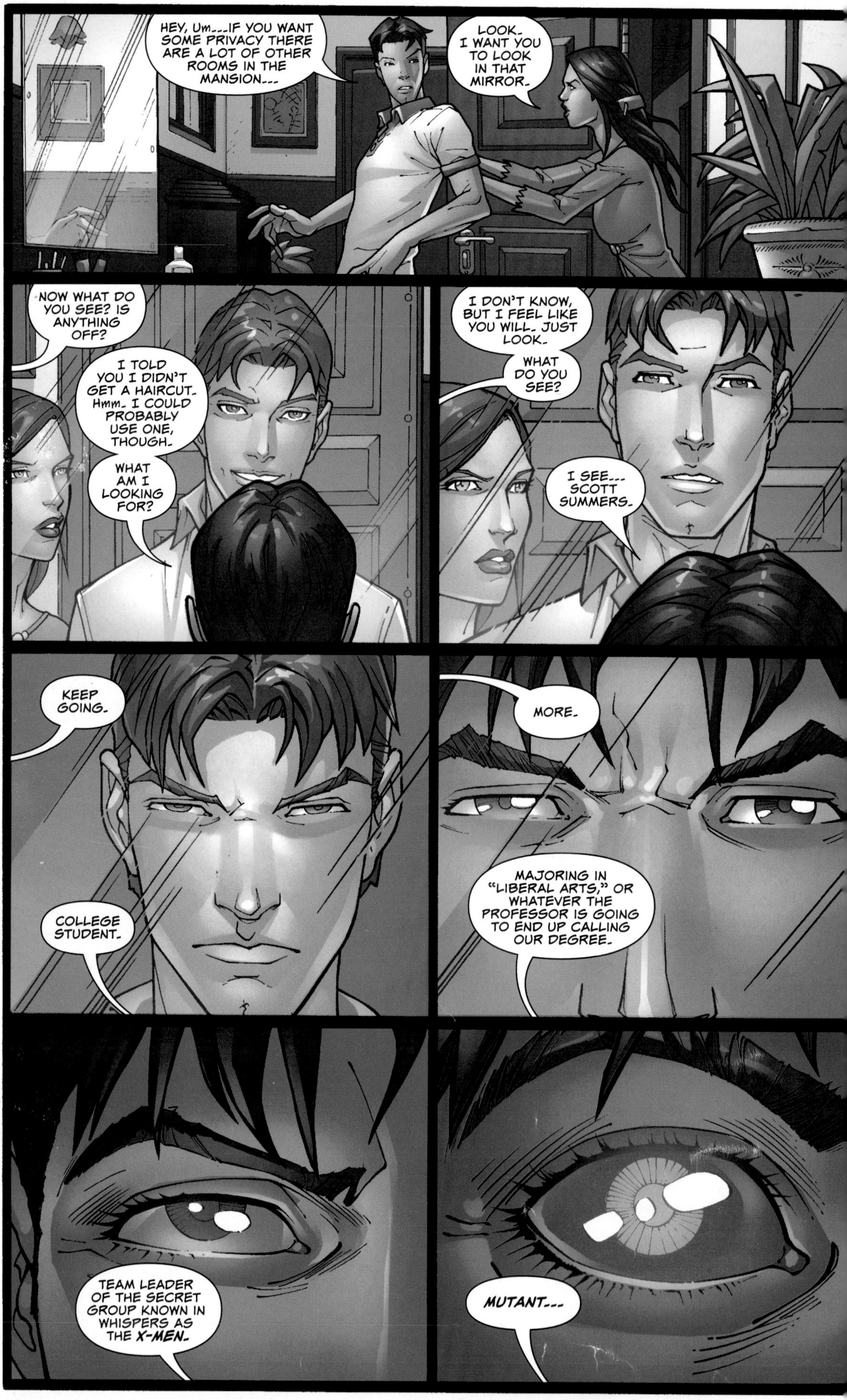
HEY, Um...IF YOU WANT SOME PRIVACY THERE ARE A LOT OF OTHER ROOMS IN THE MANSION...
LOOK. I WANT YOU TO LOOK IN THAT MIRROR.
NOW WHAT DO YOU SEE? IS ANYTHING OFF?
I TOLD YOU I DIDN'T GET A HAIRCUT. Hmm. I COULD PROBABLY USE ONE, THOUGH.
WHAT AM I LOOKING FOR?
I DON'T KNOW, BUT I FEEL LIKE YOU WILL. JUST LOOK.
WHAT DO YOU SEE?
I SEE... SCOTT SUMMERS.
KEEP GOING.
COLLEGE STUDENT.
MORE.
MAJORING IN "LIBERAL ARTS," OR WHATEVER THE PROFESSOR IS GOING TO END UP CALLING OUR DEGREE.
TEAM LEADER OF THE SECRET GROUP KNOWN IN WHISPERS AS THE X-MEN.
MUTANT...

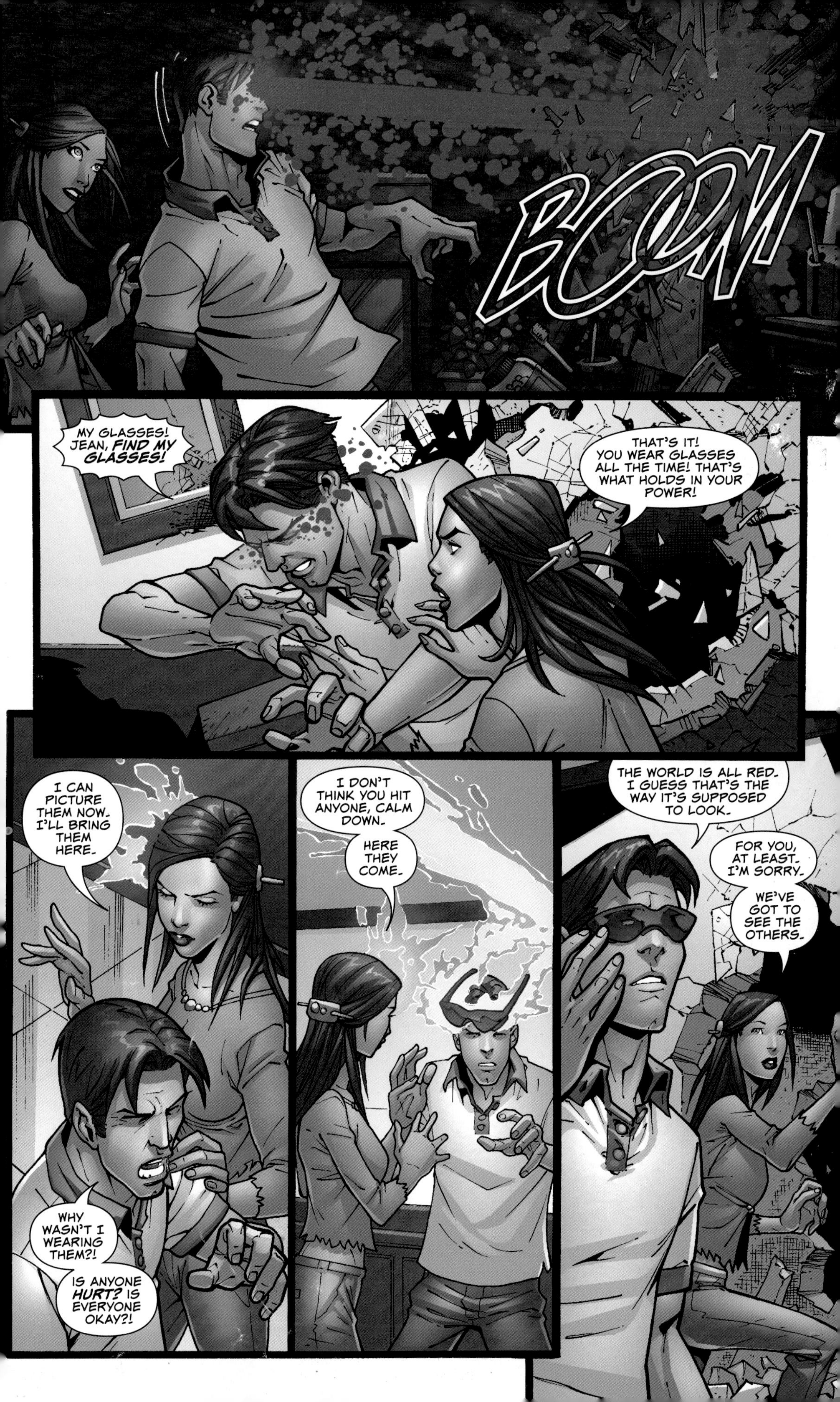
BOOM
MY GLASSES! JEAN, FIND MY GLASSES!
THAT'S IT! YOU WEAR GLASSES ALL THE TIME! THAT'S WHAT HOLDS IN YOUR POWER!
I CAN PICTURE THEM NOW. I'LL BRING THEM HERE.
WHY WASN'T I WEARING THEM?!
IS ANYONE HURT? IS EVERYONE OKAY?!
I DON'T THINK YOU HIT ANYONE, CALM DOWN.
HERE THEY COME.
THE WORLD IS ALL RED. I GUESS THAT'S THE WAY IT'S SUPPOSED TO LOOK.
FOR YOU, AT LEAST. I'M SORRY.
WE'VE GOT TO SEE THE OTHERS.

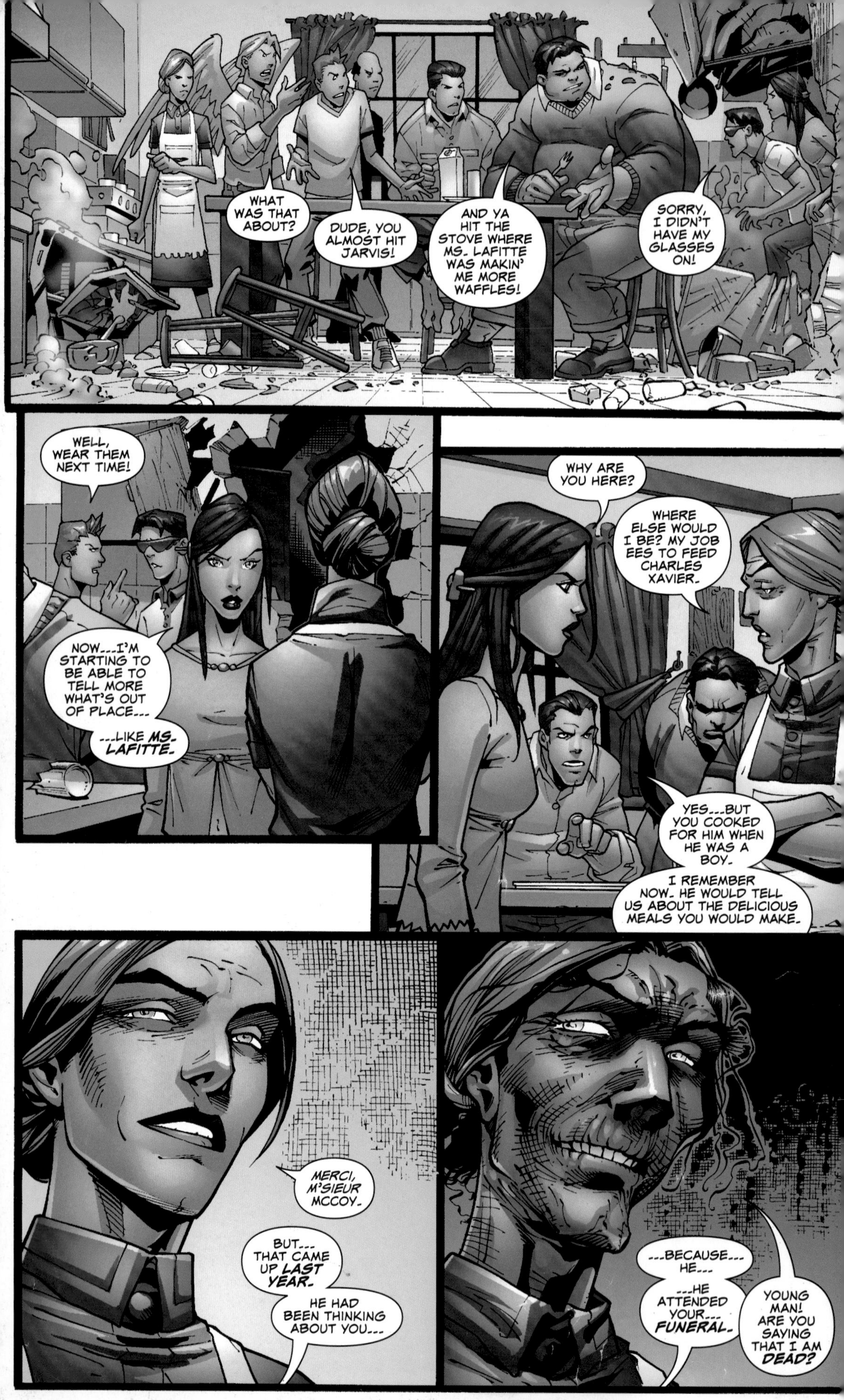
WHAT WAS THAT ABOUT?
DUDE, YOU ALMOST HIT JARVIS!
AND YA HIT THE STOVE WHERE MS. LAFITTE WAS MAKIN' ME MORE WAFFLES!
SORRY, I DIDN'T HAVE MY GLASSES ON!
WELL, WEAR THEM NEXT TIME!
NOW... I'M STARTING TO BE ABLE TO TELL MORE WHAT'S OUT OF PLACE...
...LIKE MS. LAFITTE.
WHY ARE YOU HERE?
WHERE ELSE WOULD I BE? MY JOB EES TO FEED CHARLES XAVIER.
YES... BUT YOU COOKED FOR HIM WHEN HE WAS A BOY.
I REMEMBER NOW. HE WOULD TELL US ABOUT THE DELICIOUS MEALS YOU WOULD MAKE.
MERCI, M'SIEUR MCCOY.
BUT... THAT CAME UP LAST YEAR.
HE HAD BEEN THINKING ABOUT YOU...
...BECAUSE... HE...
...HE ATTENDED YOUR... FUNERAL.
YOUNG MAN! ARE YOU SAYING THAT I AM DEAD?

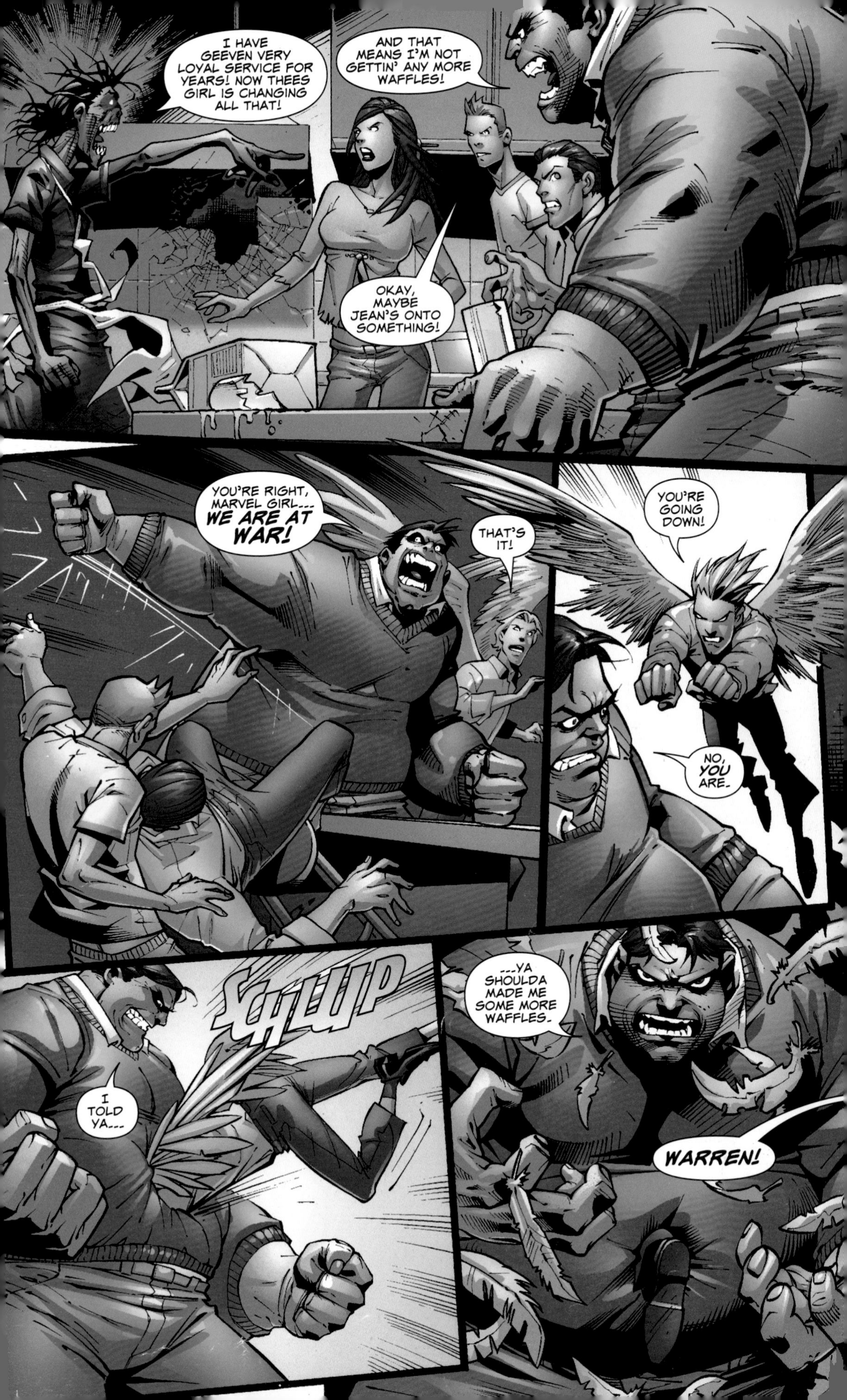
I HAVE GEEVEN VERY LOYAL SERVICE FOR YEARS! NOW THEES GIRL IS CHANGING ALL THAT!
AND THAT MEANS I'M NOT GETTIN' ANY MORE WAFFLES!
OKAY, MAYBE JEAN'S ONTO SOMETHING!
YOU'RE RIGHT, MARVEL GIRL... WE ARE AT WAR!
THAT'S IT!
YOU'RE GOING DOWN!
NO, YOU ARE.
SCHLUP
I TOLD YA...
...YA SHOULDA MADE ME SOME MORE WAFFLES.
WARREN!

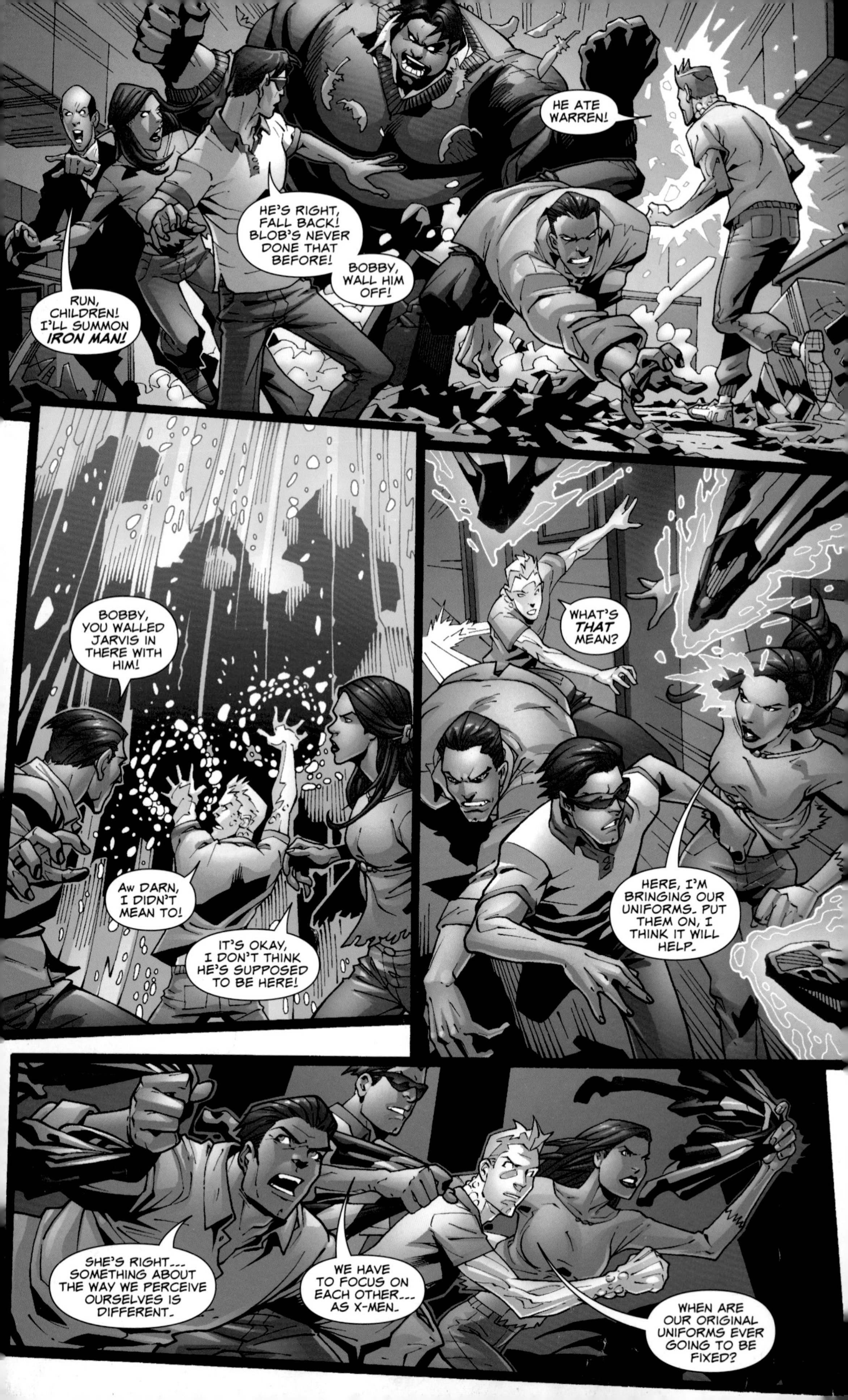
HE ATE WARREN!
HE'S RIGHT, FALL BACK! BLOB'S NEVER DONE THAT BEFORE!
BOBBY, WALL HIM OFF!
RUN, CHILDREN! I'LL SUMMON IRON MAN!
BOBBY, YOU WALLED JARVIS IN THERE WITH HIM!
Aw DARN, I DIDN'T MEAN TO!
IT'S OKAY, I DON'T THINK HE'S SUPPOSED TO BE HERE!
WHAT'S THAT MEAN?
HERE, I'M BRINGING OUR UNIFORMS. PUT THEM ON, I THINK IT WILL HELP.
SHE'S RIGHT... SOMETHING ABOUT THE WAY WE PERCEIVE OURSELVES IS DIFFERENT.
WE HAVE TO FOCUS ON EACH OTHER... AS X-MEN.
WHEN ARE OUR ORIGINAL UNIFORMS EVER GOING TO BE FIXED?

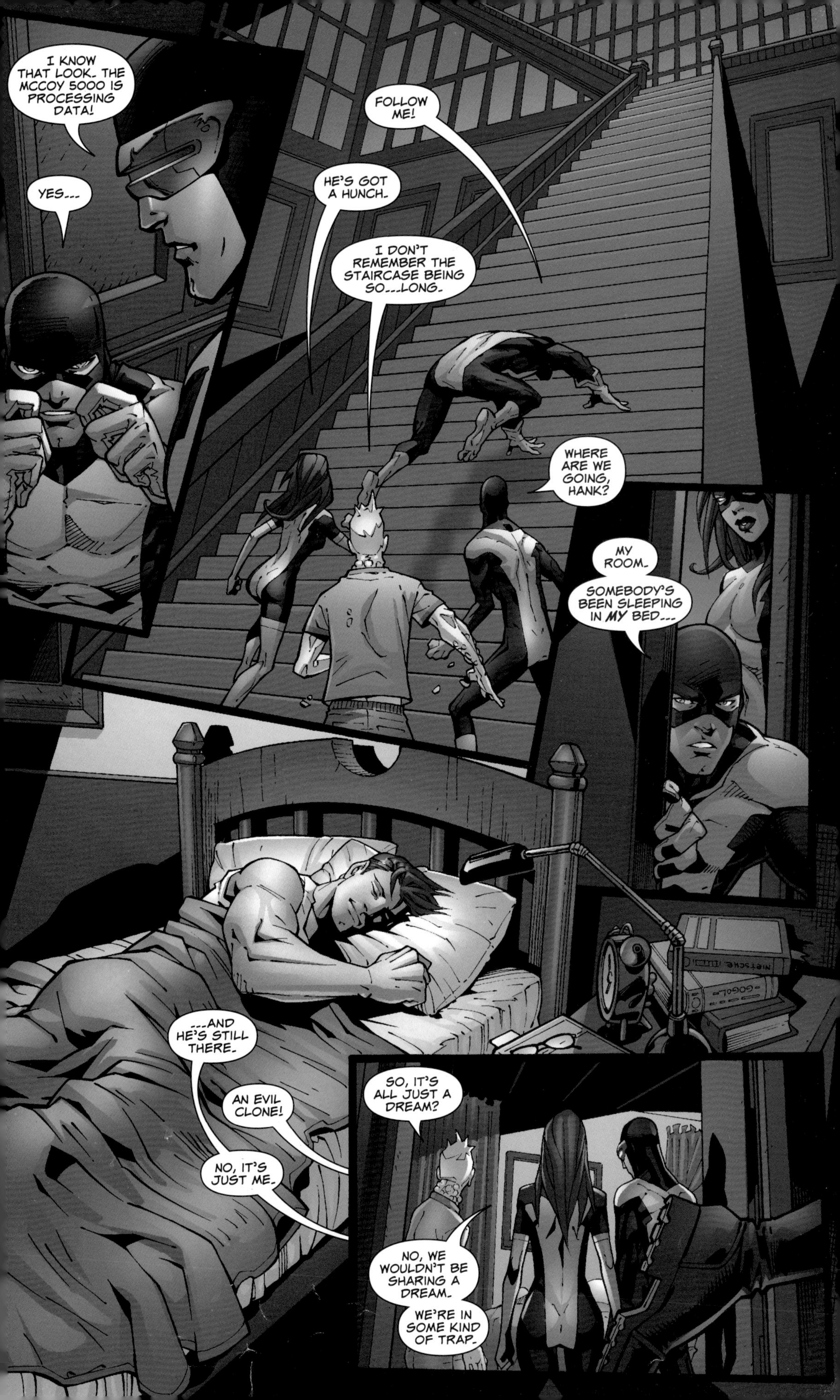
I KNOW THAT LOOK. THE MCCOY 5000 IS PROCESSING DATA!
YES...
FOLLOW ME!
HE'S GOT A HUNCH.
I DON'T REMEMBER THE STAIRCASE BEING SO...LONG.
WHERE ARE WE GOING, HANK?
MY ROOM.
SOMEBODY'S BEEN SLEEPING IN *MY* BED...
NIETSCHE
GOGOL
...AND HE'S STILL THERE.
AN EVIL CLONE!
NO, IT'S JUST ME.
SO, IT'S ALL JUST A DREAM?
NO, WE WOULDN'T BE SHARING A DREAM.
WE'RE IN SOME KIND OF TRAP.

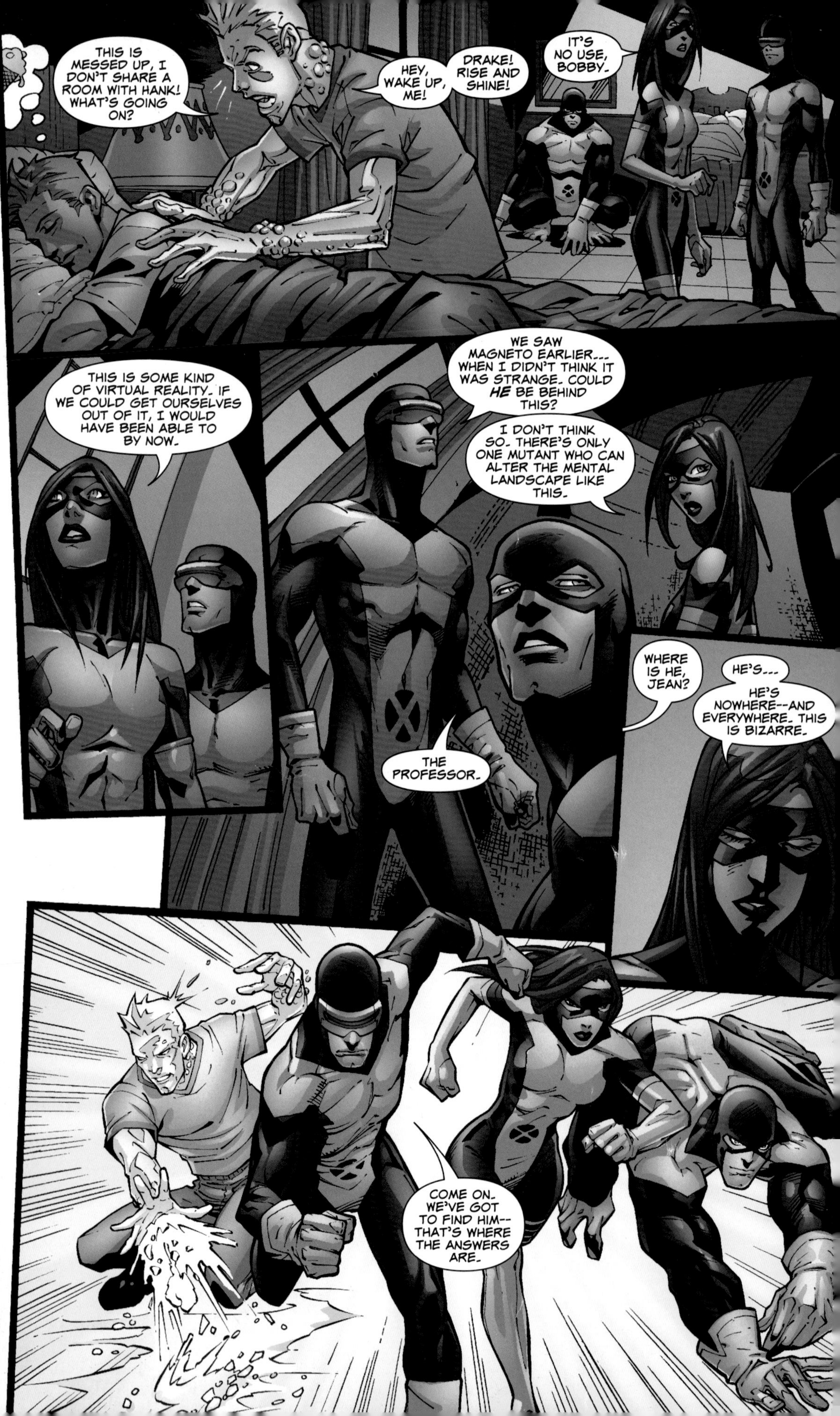
THIS IS MESSED UP, I DON'T SHARE A ROOM WITH HANK! WHAT'S GOING ON?
HEY, WAKE UP, ME!
DRAKE! RISE AND SHINE!
IT'S NO USE, BOBBY.
THIS IS SOME KIND OF VIRTUAL REALITY. IF WE COULD GET OURSELVES OUT OF IT, I WOULD HAVE BEEN ABLE TO BY NOW.
WE SAW MAGNETO EARLIER... WHEN I DIDN'T THINK IT WAS STRANGE. COULD HE BE BEHIND THIS?
I DON'T THINK SO. THERE'S ONLY ONE MUTANT WHO CAN ALTER THE MENTAL LANDSCAPE LIKE THIS.
THE PROFESSOR.
WHERE IS HE, JEAN?
HE'S...
HE'S NOWHERE--AND EVERYWHERE. THIS IS BIZARRE.
COME ON. WE'VE GOT TO FIND HIM-- THAT'S WHERE THE ANSWERS ARE.

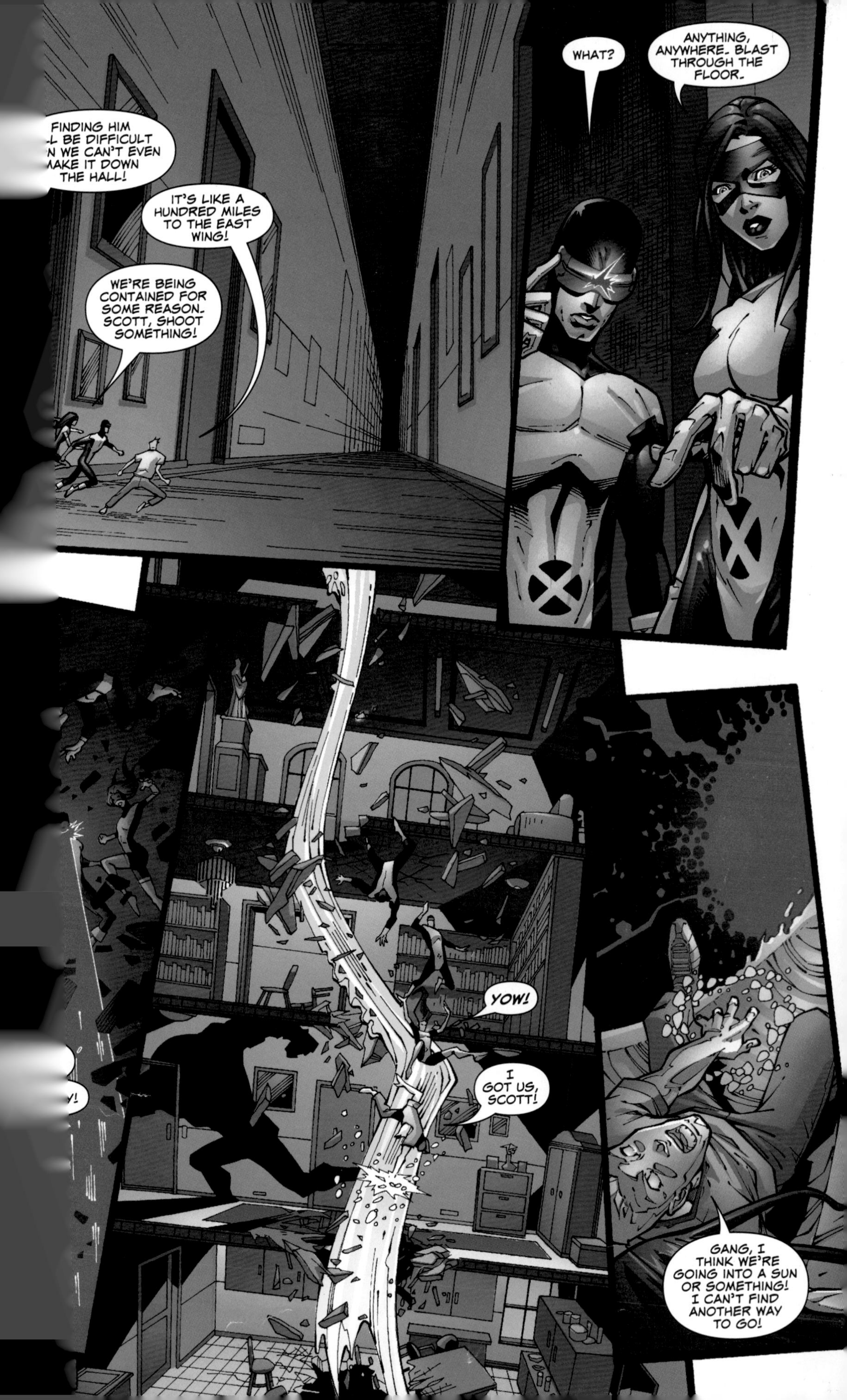
FINDING HIM -L BE DIFFICULT N WE CAN'T EVEN MAKE IT DOWN THE HALL!
IT'S LIKE A HUNDRED MILES TO THE EAST WING!
WE'RE BEING CONTAINED FOR SOME REASON. SCOTT, SHOOT SOMETHING!
WHAT?
ANYTHING, ANYWHERE. BLAST THROUGH THE FLOOR.
YOW!
I GOT US, SCOTT!
GANG, I THINK WE'RE GOING INTO A SUN OR SOMETHING! I CAN'T FIND ANOTHER WAY TO GO!

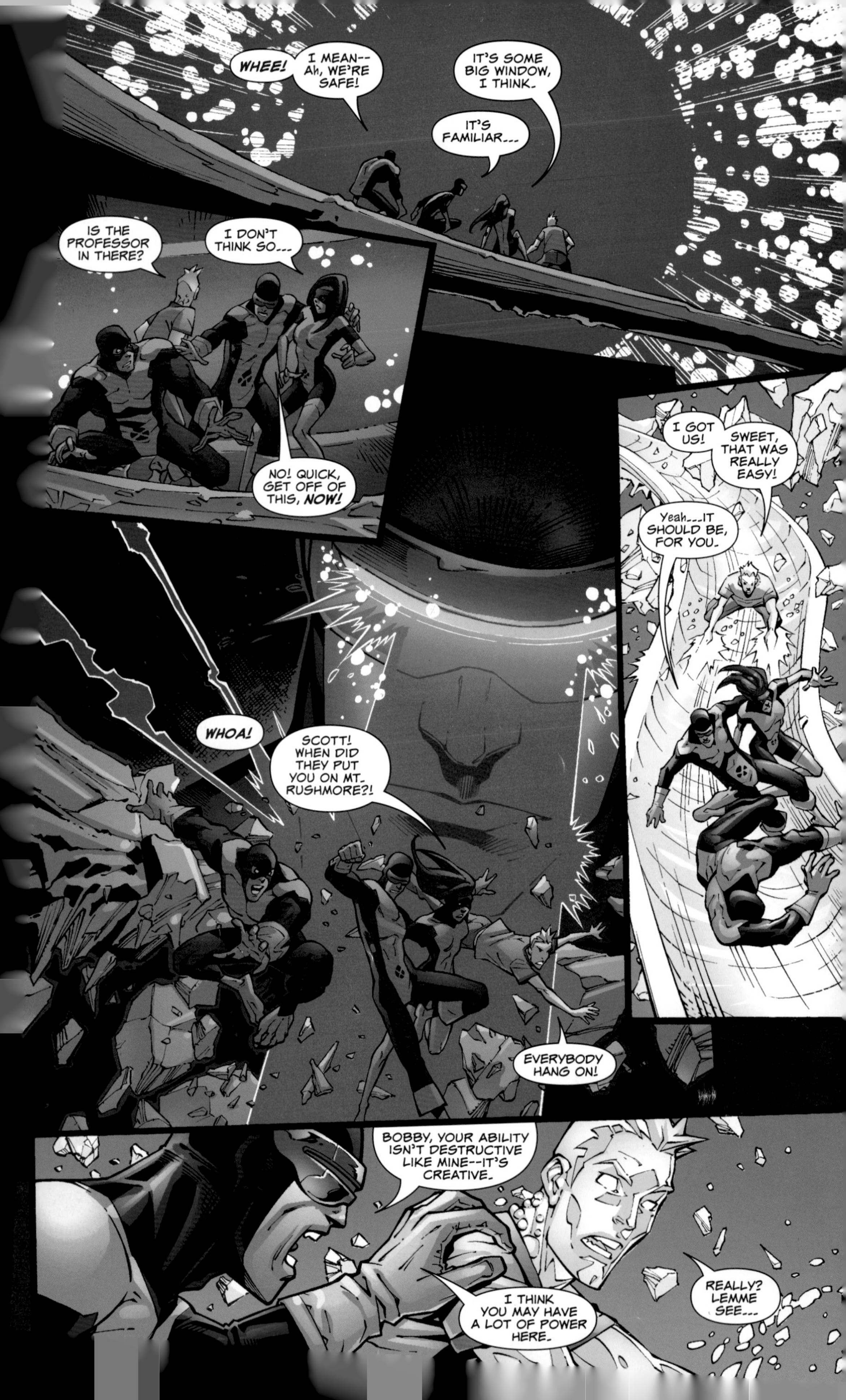
WHEE!
I MEAN-- Ah, WE'RE SAFE!
IT'S SOME BIG WINDOW, I THINK.
IT'S FAMILIAR...
IS THE PROFESSOR IN THERE?
I DON'T THINK SO...
NO! QUICK, GET OFF OF THIS, NOW!
WHOA!
SCOTT! WHEN DID THEY PUT YOU ON MT. RUSHMORE?!
EVERYBODY HANG ON!
I GOT US!
SWEET, THAT WAS REALLY EASY!
Yeah...IT SHOULD BE, FOR YOU.
BOBBY, YOUR ABILITY ISN'T DESTRUCTIVE LIKE MINE--IT'S CREATIVE.
I THINK YOU MAY HAVE A LOT OF POWER HERE.
REALLY? LEMME SEE...

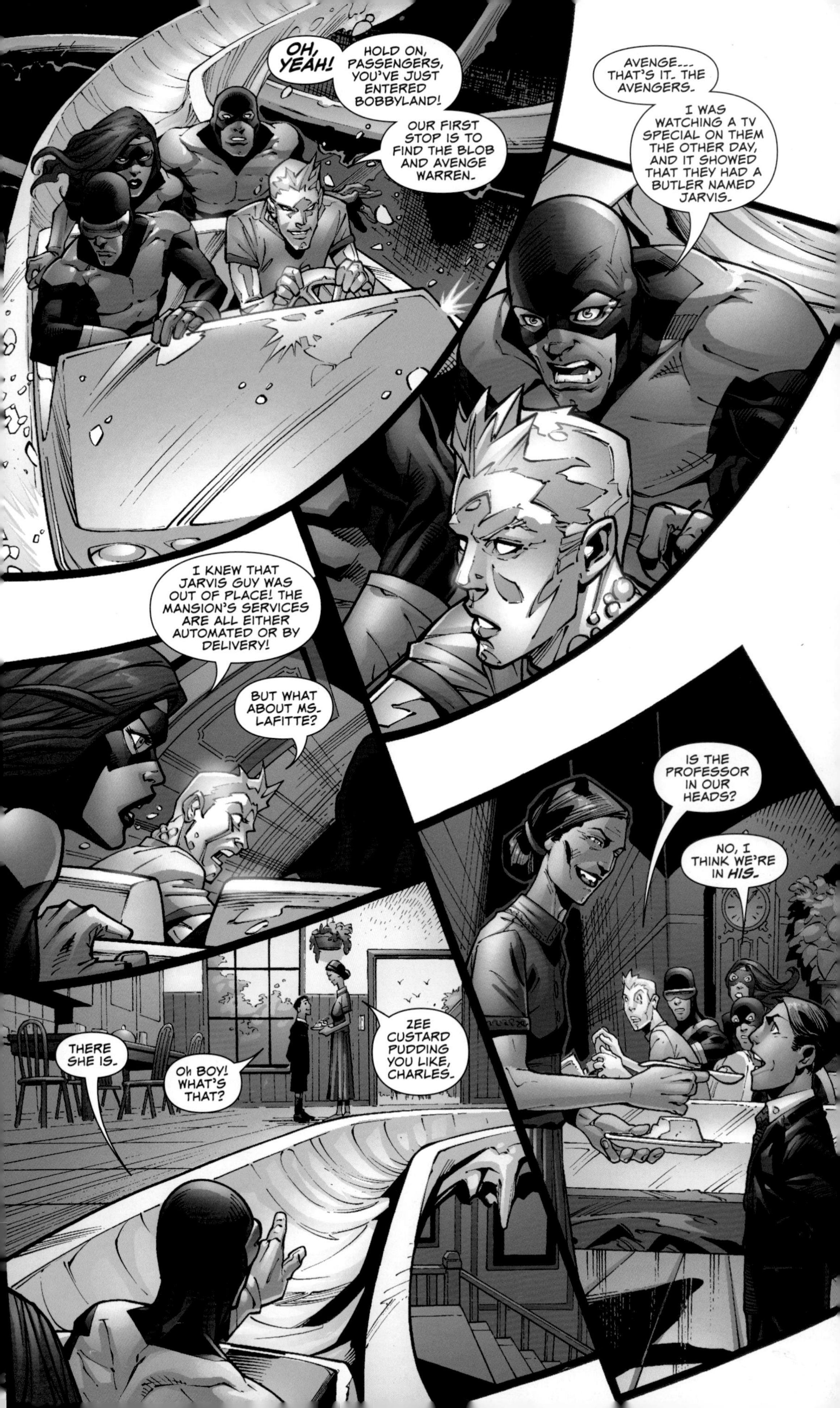
OH, YEAH!
HOLD ON, PASSENGERS, YOU'VE JUST ENTERED BOBBYLAND!
OUR FIRST STOP IS TO FIND THE BLOB AND AVENGE WARREN.
AVENGE... THAT'S IT. THE AVENGERS.
I WAS WATCHING A TV SPECIAL ON THEM THE OTHER DAY, AND IT SHOWED THAT THEY HAD A BUTLER NAMED JARVIS.
I KNEW THAT JARVIS GUY WAS OUT OF PLACE! THE MANSION'S SERVICES ARE ALL EITHER AUTOMATED OR BY DELIVERY!
BUT WHAT ABOUT MS. LAFITTE?
THERE SHE IS.
Oh BOY! WHAT'S THAT?
ZEE CUSTARD PUDDING YOU LIKE, CHARLES.
IS THE PROFESSOR IN OUR HEADS?
NO, I THINK WE'RE IN HIS.

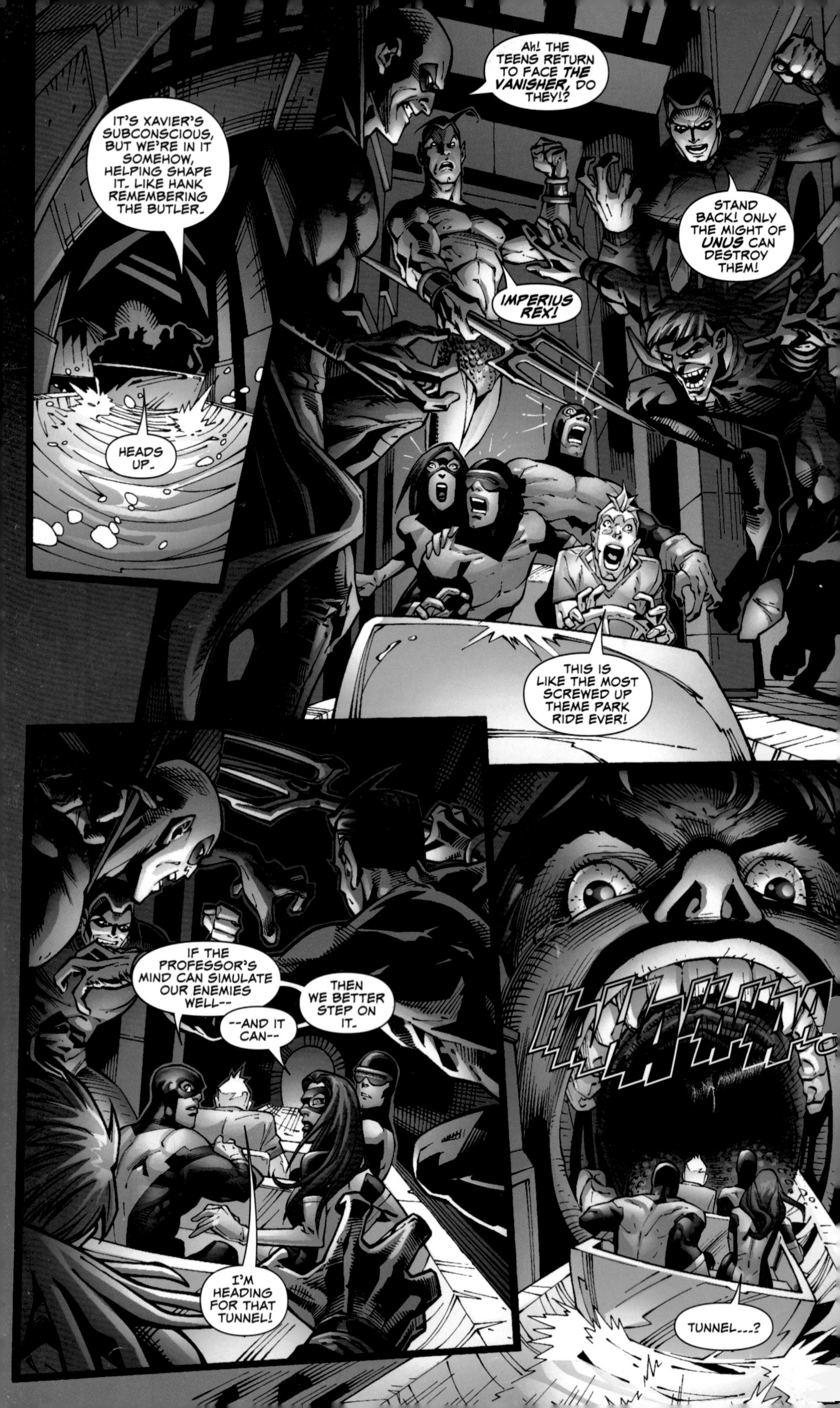

IT'S XAVIER'S SUBCONSCIOUS, BUT WE'RE IN IT SOMEHOW, HELPING SHAPE IT. LIKE HANK REMEMBERING THE BUTLER.
HEADS UP.
AH! THE TEENS RETURN TO FACE THE VANISHER, DO THEY!?
IMPERIUS REX!
STAND BACK! ONLY THE MIGHT OF UNUS CAN DESTROY THEM!
THIS IS LIKE THE MOST SCREWED UP THEME PARK RIDE EVER!
IF THE PROFESSOR'S MIND CAN SIMULATE OUR ENEMIES WELL--
--AND IT CAN--
THEN WE BETTER STEP ON IT.
I'M HEADING FOR THAT TUNNEL!
TUNNEL...?

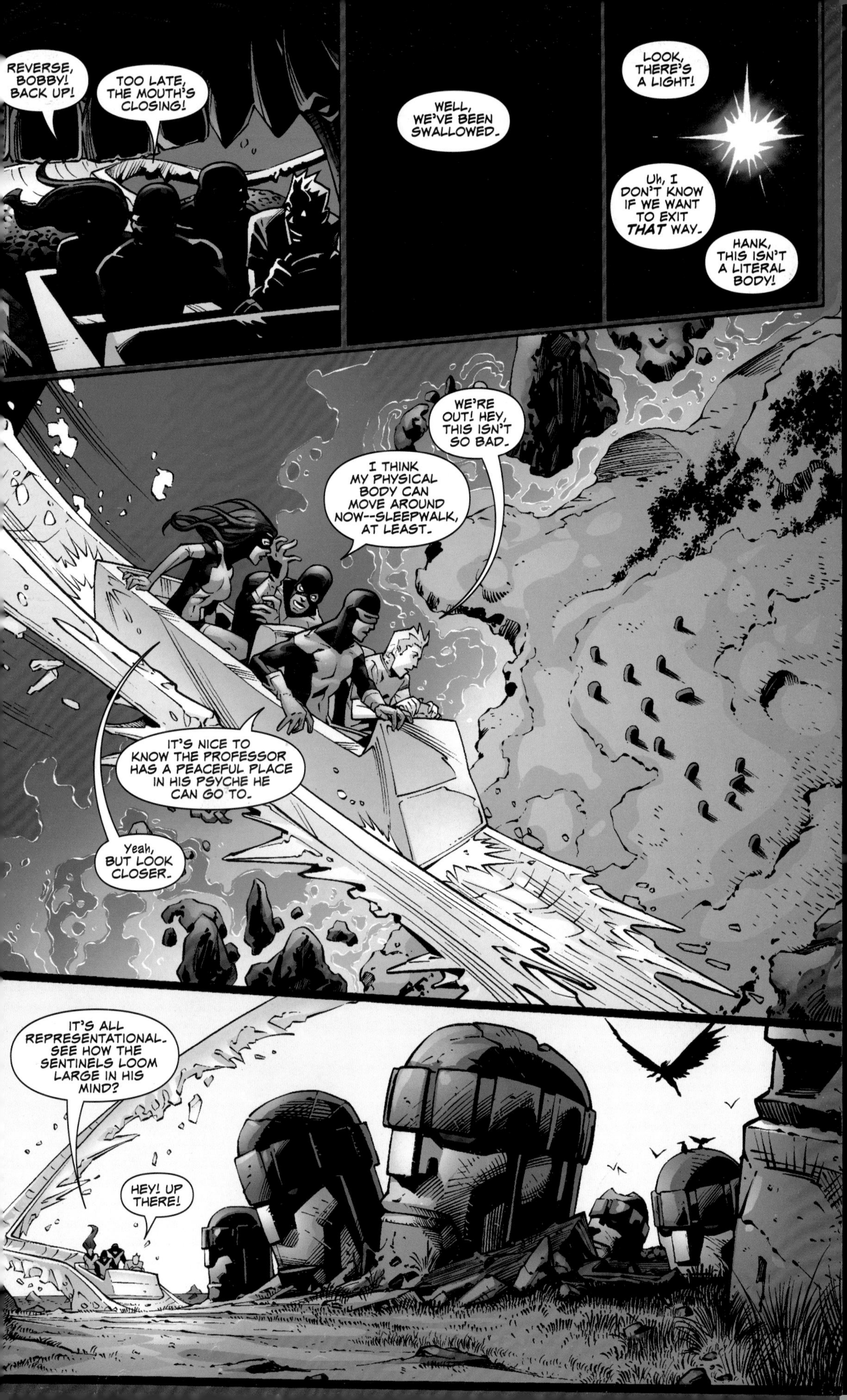
REVERSE, BOBBY! BACK UP!
TOO LATE, THE MOUTH'S CLOSING!
WELL, WE'VE BEEN SWALLOWED.
LOOK, THERE'S A LIGHT!
Uh, I DON'T KNOW IF WE WANT TO EXIT THAT WAY.
HANK, THIS ISN'T A LITERAL BODY!
WE'RE OUT! HEY, THIS ISN'T SO BAD.
I THINK MY PHYSICAL BODY CAN MOVE AROUND NOW--SLEEPWALK, AT LEAST.
IT'S NICE TO KNOW THE PROFESSOR HAS A PEACEFUL PLACE IN HIS PSYCHE HE CAN GO TO.
Yeah, BUT LOOK CLOSER.
IT'S ALL REPRESENTATIONAL. SEE HOW THE SENTINELS LOOM LARGE IN HIS MIND?
HEY! UP THERE!

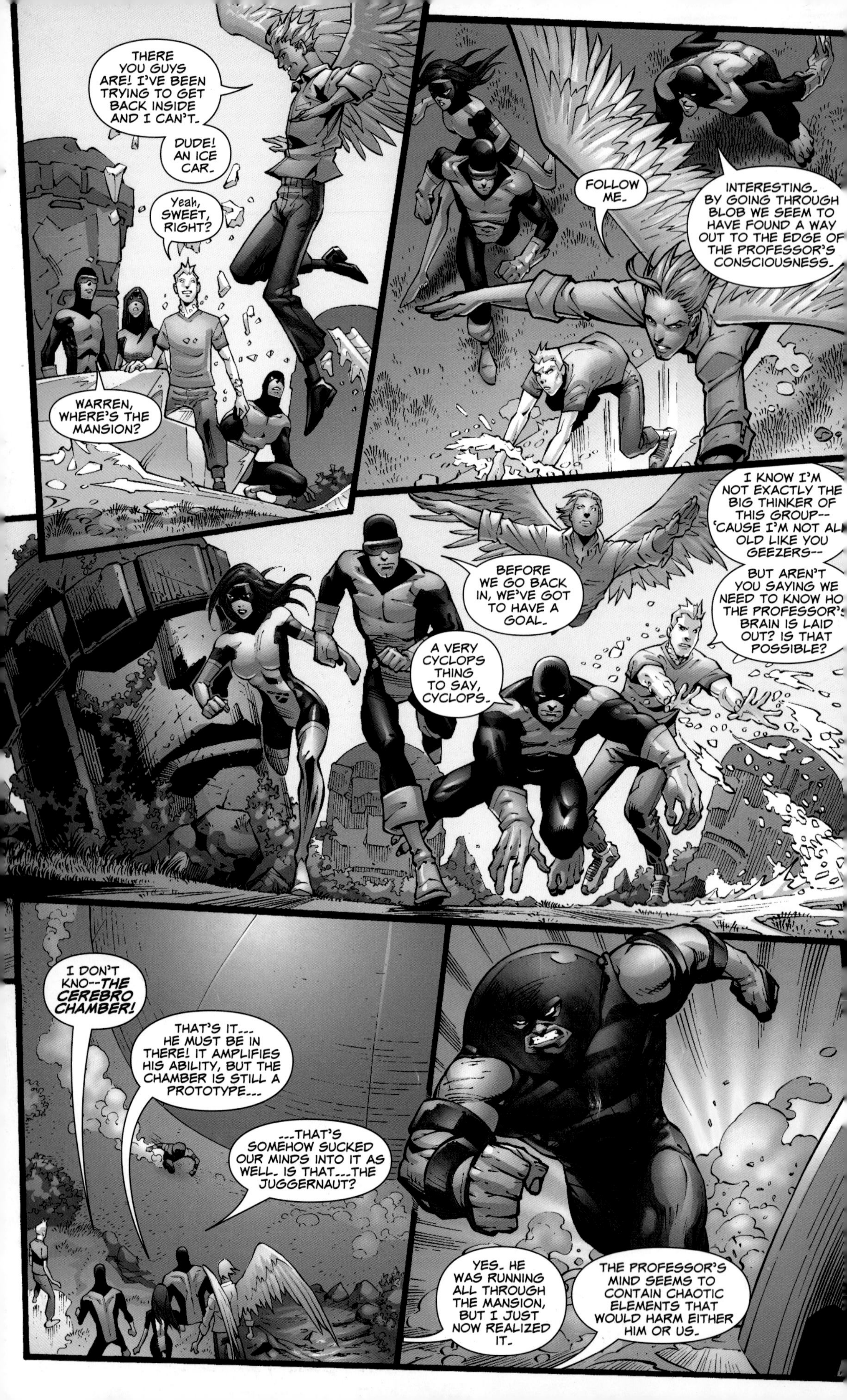

THERE YOU GUYS ARE! I'VE BEEN TRYING TO GET BACK INSIDE AND I CAN'T.
DUDE! AN ICE CAR.
Yeah, SWEET, RIGHT?
WARREN, WHERE'S THE MANSION?
FOLLOW ME.
INTERESTING. BY GOING THROUGH BLOB WE SEEM TO HAVE FOUND A WAY OUT TO THE EDGE OF THE PROFESSOR'S CONSCIOUSNESS.
BEFORE WE GO BACK IN, WE'VE GOT TO HAVE A GOAL.
I KNOW I'M NOT EXACTLY THE BIG THINKER OF THIS GROUP-- 'CAUSE I'M NOT AL OLD LIKE YOU GEEZERS--
BUT AREN'T YOU SAYING WE NEED TO KNOW HO THE PROFESSOR'S BRAIN IS LAID OUT? IS THAT POSSIBLE?
A VERY CYCLOPS THING TO SAY, CYCLOPS.
I DON'T KNO--*THE CEREBRO CHAMBER!*
THAT'S IT... HE MUST BE IN THERE! IT AMPLIFIES HIS ABILITY, BUT THE CHAMBER IS STILL A PROTOTYPE...
...THAT'S SOMEHOW SUCKED OUR MINDS INTO IT AS WELL. IS THAT...THE JUGGERNAUT?
YES. HE WAS RUNNING ALL THROUGH THE MANSION, BUT I JUST NOW REALIZED IT.
THE PROFESSOR'S MIND SEEMS TO CONTAIN CHAOTIC ELEMENTS THAT WOULD HARM EITHER HIM OR US.

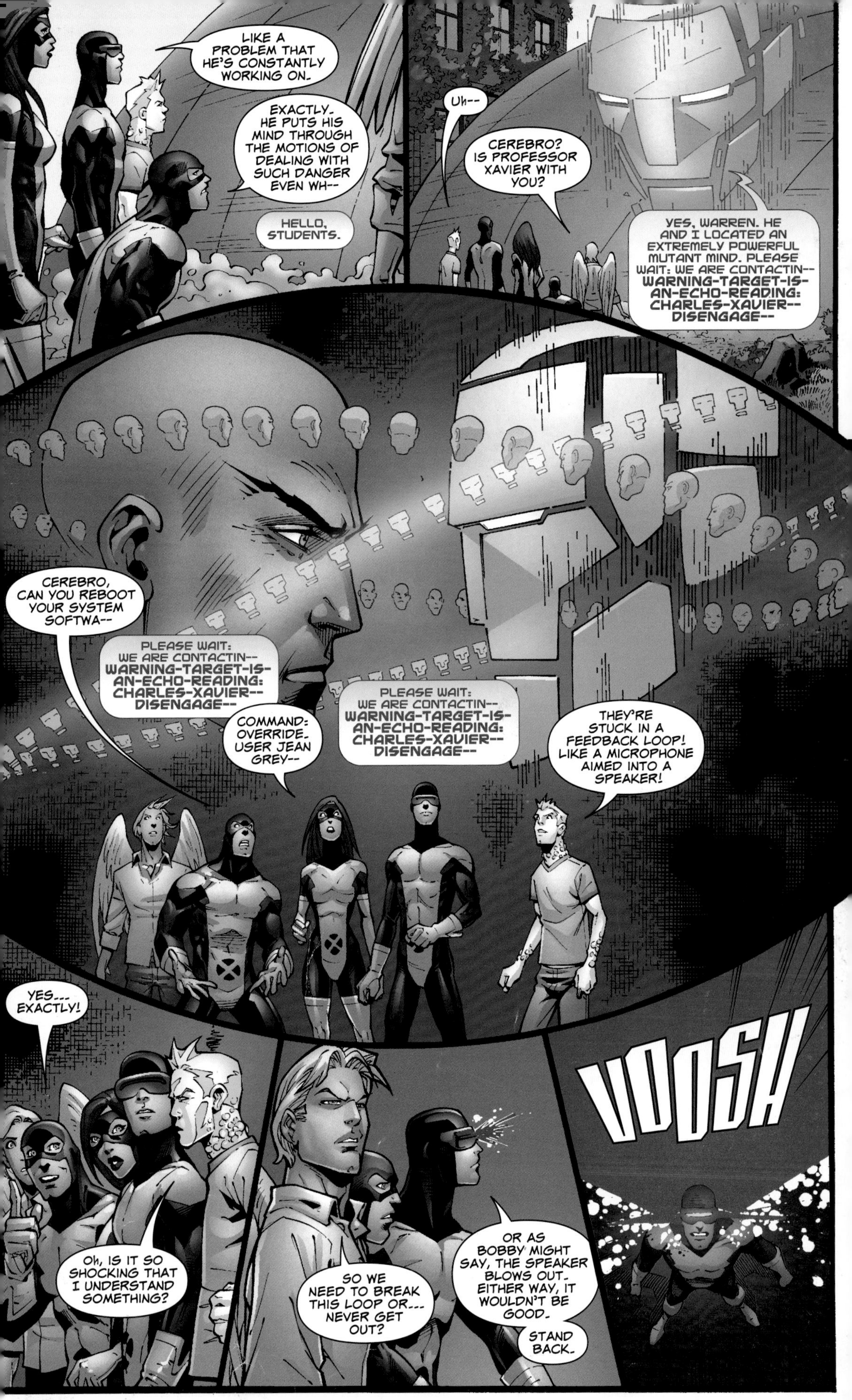

LIKE A PROBLEM THAT HE'S CONSTANTLY WORKING ON.
EXACTLY. HE PUTS HIS MIND THROUGH THE MOTIONS OF DEALING WITH SUCH DANGER EVEN WH--
HELLO, STUDENTS.
Uh--
CEREBRO? IS PROFESSOR XAVIER WITH YOU?
YES, WARREN. HE AND I LOCATED AN EXTREMELY POWERFUL MUTANT MIND. PLEASE WAIT: WE ARE CONTACTIN-- WARNING-TARGET-IS-AN-ECHO-READING: CHARLES-XAVIER-- DISENGAGE--
CEREBRO, CAN YOU REBOOT YOUR SYSTEM SOFTWA--
PLEASE WAIT: WE ARE CONTACTIN-- WARNING-TARGET-IS-AN-ECHO-READING: CHARLES-XAVIER-- DISENGAGE--
COMMAND: OVERRIDE. USER JEAN GREY--
PLEASE WAIT: WE ARE CONTACTIN-- WARNING-TARGET-IS-AN-ECHO-READING: CHARLES-XAVIER-- DISENGAGE--
THEY'RE STUCK IN A FEEDBACK LOOP! LIKE A MICROPHONE AIMED INTO A SPEAKER!
YES... EXACTLY!
Oh, IS IT SO SHOCKING THAT I UNDERSTAND SOMETHING?
SO WE NEED TO BREAK THIS LOOP OR... NEVER GET OUT?
OR AS BOBBY MIGHT SAY, THE SPEAKER BLOWS OUT. EITHER WAY, IT WOULDN'T BE GOOD.
STAND BACK.
VOOSH

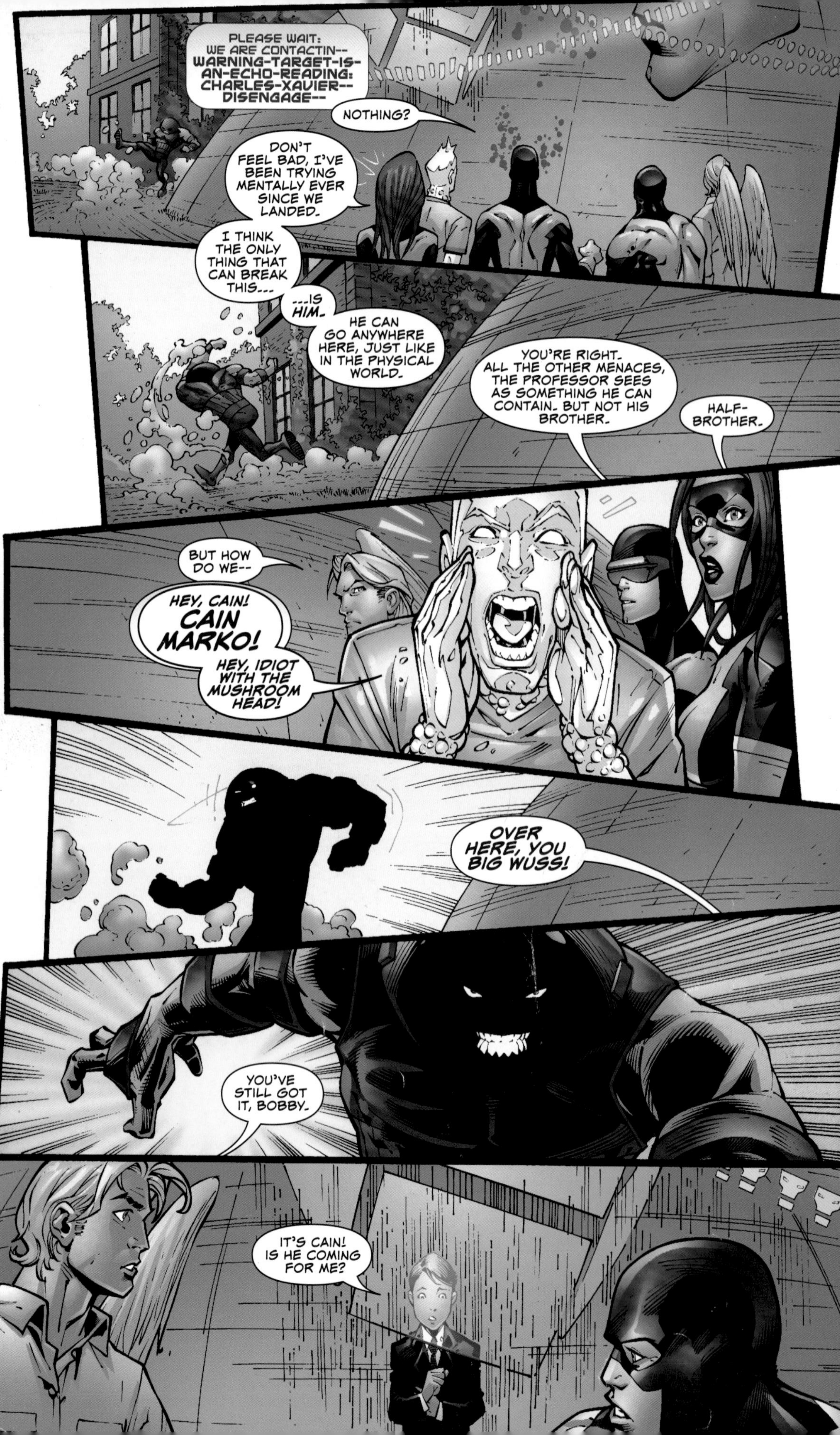

PLEASE WAIT: WE ARE CONTACTIN-- WARNING-TARGET-IS-AN-ECHO-READING: CHARLES-XAVIER-- DISENGAGE--
NOTHING?
DON'T FEEL BAD, I'VE BEEN TRYING MENTALLY EVER SINCE WE LANDED.
I THINK THE ONLY THING THAT CAN BREAK THIS...
...IS HIM.
HE CAN GO ANYWHERE HERE, JUST LIKE IN THE PHYSICAL WORLD.
YOU'RE RIGHT. ALL THE OTHER MENACES, THE PROFESSOR SEES AS SOMETHING HE CAN CONTAIN. BUT NOT HIS BROTHER.
HALF-BROTHER.
BUT HOW DO WE--
HEY, CAIN! CAIN MARKO!
HEY, IDIOT WITH THE MUSHROOM HEAD!
OVER HERE, YOU BIG WUSS!
YOU'VE STILL GOT IT, BOBBY.
IT'S CAIN! IS HE COMING FOR ME?

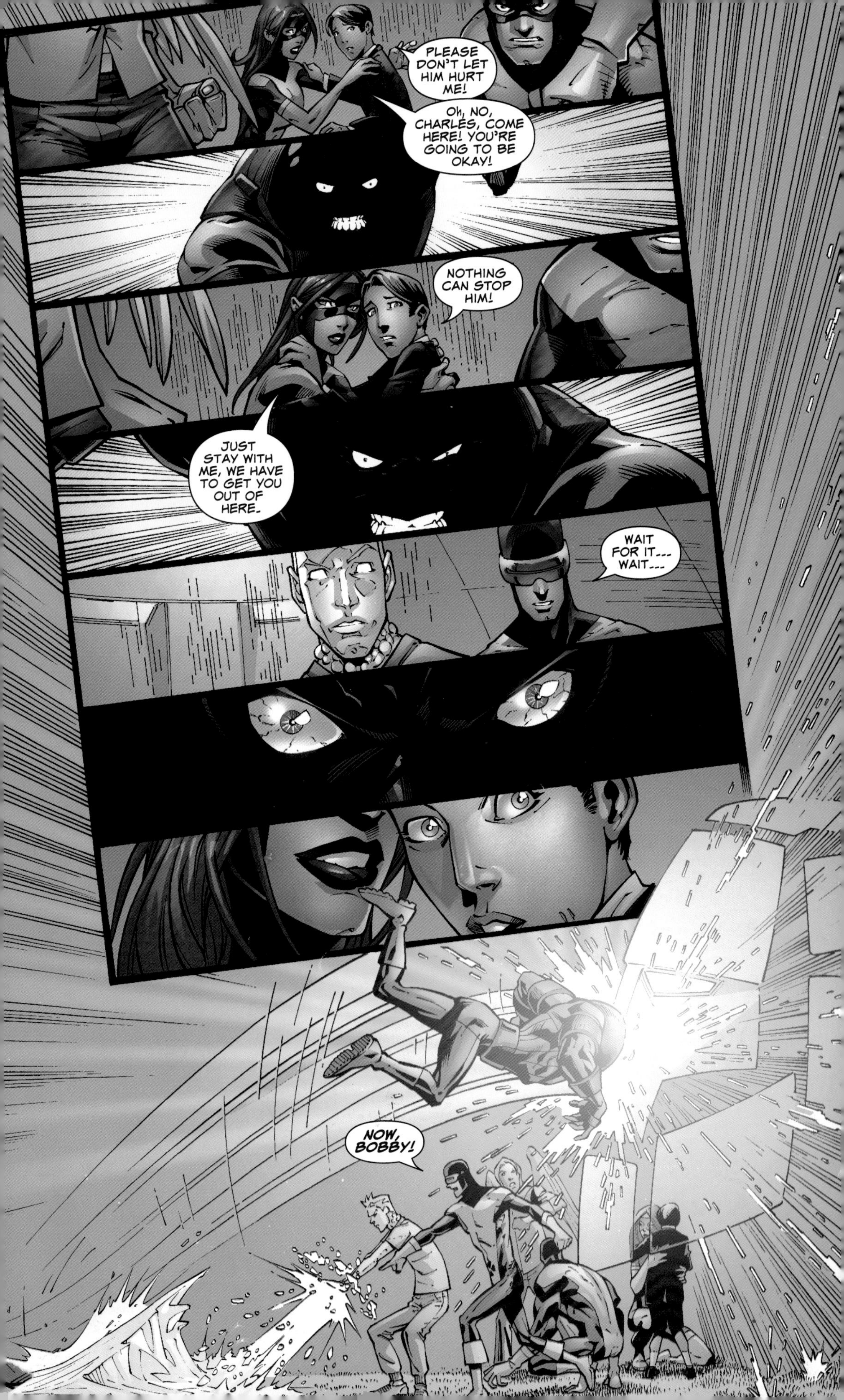
PLEASE DON'T LET HIM HURT ME!
Oh, NO, CHARLES, COME HERE! YOU'RE GOING TO BE OKAY!
NOTHING CAN STOP HIM!
JUST STAY WITH ME, WE HAVE TO GET YOU OUT OF HERE.
WAIT FOR IT... WAIT...
NOW, BOBBY!

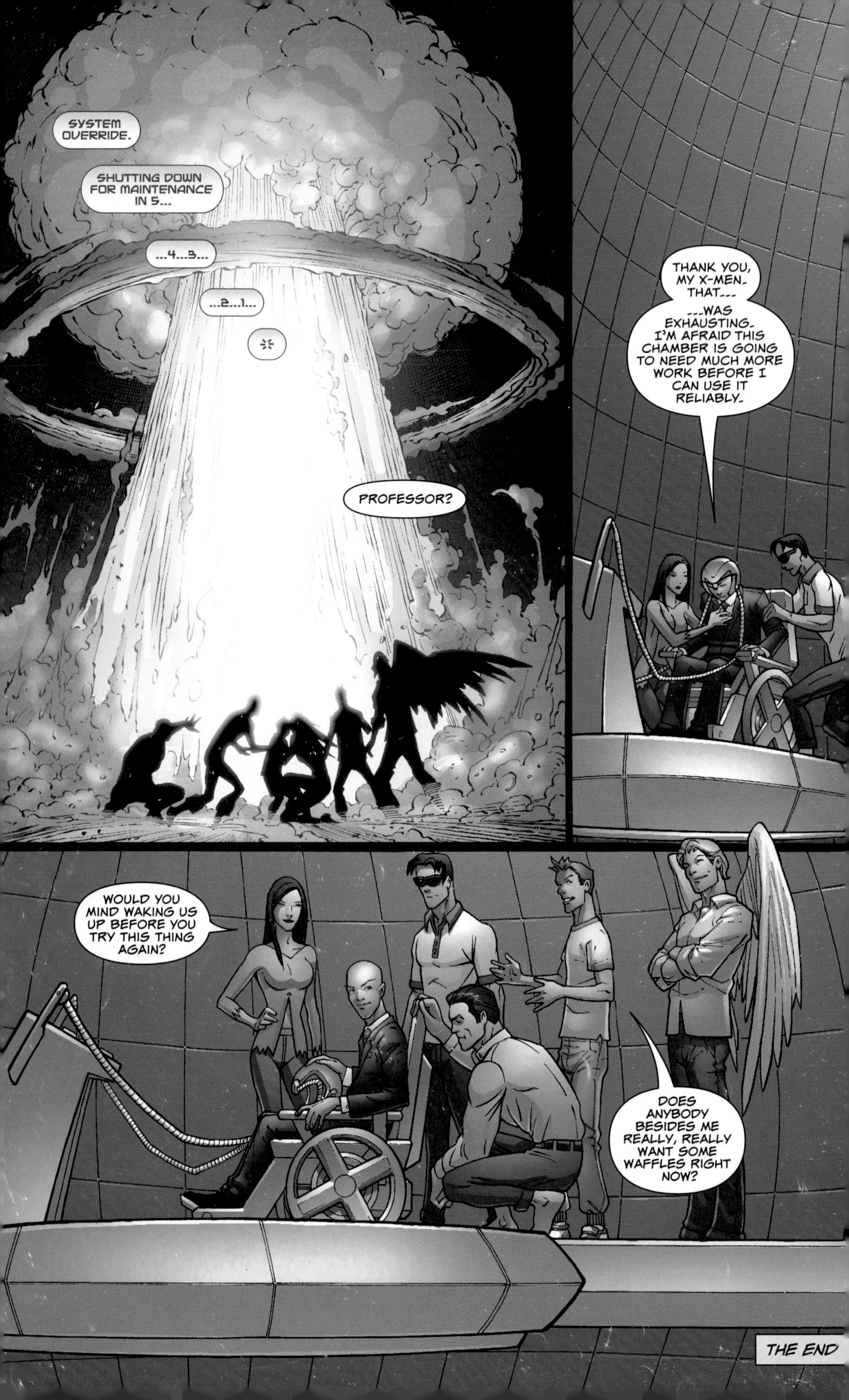
SYSTEM OVERRIDE.
SHUTTING DOWN FOR MAINTENANCE IN 5...
...4...3...
...2...1...
PROFESSOR?
THANK YOU, MY X-MEN. THAT...
...WAS EXHAUSTING. I'M AFRAID THIS CHAMBER IS GOING TO NEED MUCH MORE WORK BEFORE I CAN USE IT RELIABLY.
WOULD YOU MIND WAKING US UP BEFORE YOU TRY THIS THING AGAIN?
DOES ANYBODY BESIDES ME REALLY, REALLY WANT SOME WAFFLES RIGHT NOW?
THE END